SAM KESTREL

Coming Out on the Field

didn't help her mother, instead storming out of the house to throw rocks at an old tree stump.

Her parents didn't approve of many of the girls on her softball team. They'd made that clear more than once. Dee suspected this played a not insignificant part in their decision for her to "focus on her studies." Whenever she pressed them as to why they didn't approve of her teammates, her dad would mumble something about bad influences and her mom about them being unladylike.

Dee's first name was really Daphne, which she'd hated forever. Despite knowing this, her parents insisted on calling her by her first name, even after she started telling everyone her name was Dee back in middle school. She had long blonde hair which her parents were sure to compliment her on frequently, especially when she hinted she wanted to get it cut.

Now, as she sat in her car with the window rolled down and looked out at the field, she realized two things. First, most of the players on her new team seemed older than her by at least ten years. Second, a familiar feeling came over her, one she hadn't experienced since her last few softball games. A warmth spread throughout her entire body and with it a sense of being home. She didn't understand it, shrugging it off as she exited her car.

Out on the field, Mannie elbowed Sara. "Look who's here."

Sara glanced over toward the parking lot. A girl with long, blonde hair pulled back into a pigtail approached the field carrying a glove and cleats.

"Be nice," Sara said.

"Don't ya think she might have signed up for the wrong team?" Mannie chuckled. Sporting short dark hair that matched her skin tone and three miniature hoop earrings in each ear, she was almost as far from a white, long-haired blonde young woman as one could be.

"Think of her as adding diversity to the team," Sara quipped, who was white, but definitely not blonde. Besides, it wasn't Dee's race they were referring to. She knocked shoulders with Mannie.

Mannie laughed as Sara walked over to welcome the newcomer.

"Hi, I'm Sara. Did you sign up to play with The T.O's?"

"Kind've. I mean, I signed up for the league, and they assigned me a team."

"Well, welcome. What's your name?"

"Dee."

"Dee?" Mannie said, coming up behind Sara. "Is that short for something?"

"Yeah," Dee said, not wanting to elaborate.

"What?" Mannie pressed.

Dee sighed. "Daphne."

The corner of Mannie's lip turned up, betraying her amusement.

"I wouldn't laugh, Amanda," Sara said, pushing Mannie on the shoulder and wiping the grin off her face.

Mannie pushed Sara back.

"Don't let this one bother you," Sara said to Dee. "She's all bark but no bite."

Mannie smirked at Sara before walking away.

"Come on," Sara said, "I'll introduce you. Most of us have been playing together for a few years."

Dee assumed she wouldn't be welcome, and it showed on her face.

"So," Sara said, drawing out the o, "it will be good to have some fresh blood. Relax. We have tons of fun and everyone here is really friendly. Just give it time."

Sara seemed nice and her smile genuine. Short brown hair hung in loose curls, stopping above her shoulders. She wore shorts, a t-shirt and mismatched socks—one black and one dark green.

After introductions, the team started practice.

Rusty after not playing for a year, Dee missed some grounders during batting practice and only hit the ball out of the infield three times when her time came at the plate. She apologized profusely throughout practice, rattled that she wasn't able to show these new teammates what she could do. It was unnerving to be under the spotlight. She sensed thirteen sets of eyeballs on her during every play. Perhaps that's why she struggled as much as she did.

"How long you been playing?" Rose, the team's catcher and only Latina on the team, asked at a water break near the end of practice. She wore a dark blue t-shirt with the team name, T.O., on the front.

Dee took her question as an inquiry into why she played so poorly. Her tone reflected such. "I've always played ball," she said, unable to keep the defensiveness out of her voice. But her tone changed abruptly, becoming wistful, melancholy. "Well, not my senior year.... Sorry I'm so rusty. I haven't played in over a year."

"You're fine. I asked out of curiosity, that's all. Where'd you go to school?"

"Valley High."

Rose whistled. "Hey, everyone," she called out to the team. "Dee here played for Valley High."

Dee blushed. "Don't. I didn't start much or—"

"If you were good enough to make the team, you've got some skills." Rose smiled. "Give yourself time. And don't worry about these women. They won't bother you. Unless, of course, you want them to."

Not understanding what Rose meant, but not wanting to admit it, Dee merely smiled.

At the end of practice, as most of the women were taking off their cleats and bantering back and forth, Dee noticed Sara and another player, Izzy, setting up for extra batting practice.

"Are you staying longer?" Dee asked, walking up to Sara, who stood on the pitcher's mound. Izzy waited at the plate.

"Yeah. Izzy wanted some extra batting practice. You're welcome to stay."

Dee smiled. "I'll shag." She jogged out to stand on the third-base side of second base. The sun was lower in the sky. She crouched down to avoid catching the glare in her eyes. A soft breeze blew cool air across her face. She loved this time of the day. Only towards the end of practice did she settle in and the cobwebs fall away. Now, fully warmed-up, her skills started to show. She stopped every ground ball except the ones Izzy hit along the first or third-base line.

After ten minutes, Sara called out to her. "Want to hit?"

Dee smiled. "Yeah!"

This second batting practice went much better than her first. If she'd paid attention at all to the few women who remained on the bleachers talking, she would have seen some head nods and heard positive comments about her playing ability. Ten minutes later, Izzy, having run around shagging balls with less success than Dee before her, called out that she needed to leave. Dee offered to get the rest of the balls and after thanking her, Izzy ran off, leaving Sara and Dee alone on the field.

Sara held out a bucket of balls. Dee upturned her glove, dropping in the three balls she'd picked up in the outfield.

"Feeling better?" Sara asked.

"Yeah. Thanks for letting me bat again."

They turned and walked toward the bleachers.

"No problem," Sara said. "Can I ask you a question?"

Dee ran to retrieve a ball she'd spotted against the fence. "Sure," she called over her shoulder. After jogging back to Sara and dropping the ball in the bucket, she waited for Sara to speak. They headed to the bleachers to take off their cleats.

"Why didn't you play your senior year?" Sara asked.

"My parents pressed me to quit."

"In your senior year?" Sara said, disbelief etched in her voice. "That must have been rough."

Dee nodded. The memory still hurt, and she didn't have the words to convey just how much.

"Can I ask why?"

"My grades weren't great. That's the reason they gave. But they also made it clear they didn't like many of the girls I played with."

"Do you know why?"

"No clue."

"Really?" Sara gave Dee an obvious look of incredulity.

"What?" Dee said.

Sara paused, clearly debating what to say next. She shook her head. "Nothing."

Dee's eyes squinted in a puzzled sort of way. But she said nothing. A part of her wanted to understand what she didn't. Another part worried about what Sara might say. She grabbed her cleats. "See you Thursday?"

"See you Thursday."

"Oh, one more question," Dee said, turning around to face Sara.

"Yeah?"

"What's T.O. mean? The name of the team?"

"Toaster Ovens."

Dee looked at Sara with a blank expression.

"Never mind," Sara said.

Chapter 2

Over the next three weeks, Dee woke up excited on Tuesday and Thursday mornings, thinking of the day's practice. She felt more welcomed on the team, or perhaps she'd always been welcomed, and her self-consciousness finally took a back seat. She also watched the other players with intrigue. Two of the women were clearly a couple. At first, she thought they were just really good friends. But then they kissed on the field. Sally headed out to right field and stopped in front of Georgia, who stood on first base. They kissed in passing on the lips. Georgia, facing Dee's direction, caught her watching and smiled. Dee had looked away, blushing, though she didn't know why.

From other snippets of conversation, she gathered that Rose and Izzy were also gay. Dee couldn't figure out Mannie's story. Teammates teased her about only being a top, but Dee had no idea what that meant. She figured it had something to do with sex but didn't want to admit to her cluelessness and was too embarrassed to ask. Also, Mannie presented as quite androgynous, which Dee found intriguing but also confusing.

After the third Thursday of practice, when inserting the key into her car's ignition, it finally hit her. Every single player on the team identified as a lesbian. How had she been so blind? Through her windshield, she spotted Sally and Georgia standing arm-in-arm. Mannie with her short hair and stance that made it difficult to tell her sex from behind. Short and stocky, Rose stood with legs spread apart, spitting into the dirt. She'd mentioned her girlfriend several times. Izzy, with her short brown hair buzzed on the side, spoke of different love interests, all women, almost every week, if not every practice. Similar stories could be told of the other players on the team, some quieter about it than others, but none hiding their lives. Except Sara. Sara never mentioned a girlfriend or those she'd slept with. But she'd responded to the other's banter and jokes in a way that made it clear that she, too, was a lesbian.

Lying in bed that night, Dee realized something else. Several of the players on her high school team had been gay. Well, probably still are. Definitely Taylor. She'd been out and paid for it dearly. She was one of the only lesbians, well, out lesbians, at school. If there were others, and Dee now realized there had to be others, they'd stayed under the radar after seeing how the school treated Taylor. Taunts in the corridors were common, though after she decked a boy in her junior year, people kept comments to themselves or made them behind her back and wrote their notes anonymously.

Faces of other players from her high school team flashed in her mind, those whom Dee now suspected might have been gay. Could that be the real reason her parents pushed her to quit? Of course. It seemed obvious now. So obvious, in fact, that it seemed foolish to not have realized it sooner.

Extremely homophobic, to say her parents didn't like gay people was like saying George Wallace didn't like Black people.

okay?"

"It's fine, dear."

"Why are you back so soon?"

"Just go and watch your movie," her mother said.

"But—"

"For some reason the Walters invited some faggots to dinner," her father said. "I'll need to talk to Joe about that later."

"Of course, we couldn't stay," her mother added matter-of-factly.

Dee stood in the hallway, shame welling up inside her. They'd used derogatory terms before, of course, but her best friend was in the other room, and Dee was embarrassed by her parents. Not wanting to extend the conversation any longer, Dee wheeled around and returned to the living room.

One final memory came flooding back. Of when she didn't remember. She'd snuck down the hall, intent on overhearing her parent's conversation. They'd intentionally kept their voices down, but she'd caught the words softball, lesbo and dyke. As Dee turned the key in the ignition, her eyes still on her new teammates, she had to wonder. Why'd she blocked out that conversation until now?

Chapter 3

The first game of the season proved an exciting one. Dee turned a double play in the first inning to get Mannie out of a jam after she walked two batters and earned a high five and a smile in return. In the ninth inning with the score tied at three and one out, Dee hit a single into the outfield, pushing Izzy over to third. That allowed Sara to come up, and she didn't disappoint, hitting a deep fly ball that was caught, but allowed Izzy to tag up and come home for the winning run.

Over the high fives and calls of "good job," Sara reminded the team that the barbeque started at three o'clock. "And Izzy," Sara said over the heads of the team sitting on the bleachers, "none of that store-bought potato salad."

"Yeah, yeah," Izzy said, as Mannie pushed her on the shoulder.

Always eager to be out from under her parent's eyes, Dee arrived well before everyone else, even after fretting at the store over what she should bring. She couldn't very well make something at home without her mother asking questions. Finally deciding on a watermelon, she knocked on Sara's door at two fifty.

"Sorry I'm early," Dee said as Sara opened the door. Taken by the sight of Sara's hazel eyes, Dee's eyes quickly found the ground. "Needed to get out of the house."

"No problem. Come on in."

Dee stepped over the threshold. Her body suddenly became warm. She straightened her shirt and ran a hand through her hair. They passed a bathroom, and Dee resisted the impulse to check her teeth for stray bits of food.

"Follow me," Sara said. "You can cut that up in the kitchen."

After arranging slices of watermelon on paper plates, Dee helped Sara finish setting up and volunteered to grill the chicken and hamburgers. She found it easier to be busy at parties when she didn't know people that well. And while she felt more comfortable around everyone, she was still the newbie and the age gap was something that made her self-conscious.

After an hour, however, Izzy kicked her off the grill. "Stop hiding and go mingle," she said, holding out her hand for the tongs.

With the party in full swing, Dee couldn't help but notice that nearly all of her teammates came with their girlfriends.

"Paula, this is our newest addition, Dee. Dee, this is my partner, Paula." Mannie gave Dee a side squeeze around the shoulders.

"Nice to meet you, Paula."

"She doesn't pick on you too hard, does she?" Paula asked Dee.

Dee shook her head. "No." She was a bit taken by Paula. Tall, dark and gorgeous, she wore three-inch heels and impeccably applied make up. Dee would not have thought Paula was a lesbian if she passed her on the street.

"Now, don't go hittin' on my woman," Mannie said teasingly to Dee. Only, Dee didn't realize she was kidding.

Dee's face turned red, not having realized she was staring.

15

"Nn … nn … no. Why would I—?"

Mannie busted up laughing. "Chill out, girl. You're too uptight. Go get a beer or something.

Dee wandered away, mumbling under her breath.

"Dee! Come over here." Rose was waving her over from across the yard. "Dee, this is my girlfriend, Sofia."

The two women exchanged hellos and didn't have time to say anything else before a roar rose from a crowd in the middle of the yard. Mannie seemed to be telling a good story and had everyone laughing.

A wave of heat streaked through Dee's body, threatening to make her dizzy. She struggled to catch her breath. The slightly warm, fuzzy sensation she had when at softball practice grew too hot and overbearing and threatened to overwhelm her. She made a beeline for the house, going through the back door, down the hall and into the guest bedroom, where she sat on the bed after closing the door.

With her head in her hands, realizations flew at her like rapid-fire balls out of a pitching machine. Should she laugh or cry? It was as if a dam of understanding and self-awareness broke and washed over her. Her parents' homophobia, the boyfriends she just couldn't get into, the sex she refused. How was it coming to her only now? How could she not have realized this until now? Later she'd discover that many people didn't come out until their thirties or forties, but to her, it seemed as if she'd wasted so much time. So much time unable to be truly herself.

She didn't know how long she'd been in the room when the door opened. "You okay in here?" Sara said.

Dee nodded, but her tear-splashed face said something different.

"What's wrong?" Sara asked, coming to sit next to her on the

kept a straight face. "I'm kidding. I don't know what now. Everyone's different. Maybe sit with it a bit. See how it feels to acknowledge that truth about yourself.

Dee nodded and took a bite of her chicken, which seemed to taste different from before. In a good way.

"Is there anyone you're secretly attracted to?" Sara asked. "I think we all have secret crushes we try to ignore before we come out."

Although Dee shook her head, they both understood that she was lying. Sara could tell by the shiftiness of her eyes and Dee, well, she just knew. But how to tell the person in front of you that you like her? The redness in her cheeks didn't help matters.

"You're blushing," Sara said playfully. "Why are you blushing?" The truth came to her after a moment of silence. Dee was attracted to her. Wow. This might get awkward. But not because Sara was put off. She actually found Dee attractive and had from the moment she'd walked on the field for the first practice. There were moments when Sara wondered if Dee wasn't gay, but other times, she was less confident in her assessment.

What should Sara say, if anything? Dee was in an extremely vulnerable place and at a very important moment in her life. Sara didn't want to take advantage of that. Or did she? True, Dee was eight years her junior and blonde, but hadn't an older woman eased Sara's coming out all those years ago?

Sara realized her mind had wandered. When she finally brought herself back to the present, Dee was staring at her. As the two made eye contact, Dee's eyes flitted down to Sara's lips.

Dee blushed, her eyes having betrayed a desire that blossomed with each second as she sat next to Sara. Sara with her short brown hair, button nose and hazel eyes. Sara, whom Dee watched each practice when she stood in the batter's on-deck circle, waiting for her turn at the plate. How she walked with a skip in her step, her arms relaxed at her sides. How her uniform showed off her ass nicely, hugging its tight curves.

"What do you want right now?" Sara whispered.

"I … I …" Dee couldn't bring herself to say what she wanted, but her eyes did her talking for her as they again drifted down from Sara's eyes.

Chapter 4

Sara leaned forward but stopped herself. What would others say? That she took advantage of the newbie, perhaps? Probably. Well, did she care? Before she made up her mind, she realized that the little she had leaned forward didn't go unnoticed by Dee, who leaned in as Sara silently argued with herself.

Well, I wouldn't want to leave her hanging, would I? And Sara again moved toward Dee.

Their lips brushed softly. Once, twice, three times. The two women broke apart to gaze at one another. Sara gave Dee a little smile. After all, she was relaxed. It wasn't her first time. She understood it was probably much different for Dee.

Far from relaxed, Dee felt nervous and excited. Her body tingled with anticipation and an unfamiliar sensation blossomed between her legs. Sure, she'd masturbated. But when you're supposed to like boys, but don't, and aren't willing to admit you like girls, and aren't supposed to, it's hard to have fantasies that aren't fraught with shame or interrupted by internal arguments and admonitions.

Now the full awakening of Dee's sexuality was fast forwarded.

She found she couldn't think and didn't want to. Consequences be damned. A beautiful woman sat in front of her, and she'd just freed herself from the constraints of others' homophobia. Had she known the bindings, tattered and old, would need so little to break apart, might she not have broken free sooner?

Dee returned Sara's smile, focusing on Sara's face: her smile, those eyes, patient but also ... What else was there? Desire perhaps. Or maybe she only wanted to see that. Again, Dee leaned forward and Sara mirrored her movements. This time, they kissed more intensely, and neither broke away. Instead, their tongues flitted against one another, playfully at first, but this shifted as desire took over and demanded more. Soon they were wrapped in each other's arms, holding one another tight as they made out, outwardly demonstrating the depths of their inner longing.

Sara hadn't spent the last weeks pining for Dee. She'd noticed her, sure, and wondered if she might not be struggling with her sexuality. No, for Sara, this was more of an immediate desire, or perhaps a desire of opportunity, brought on by the conditions of the moment. She wasn't seeing anyone, nor was there anyone in whom she had even the slightest interest. But she liked sex just as much, if not more than the next person, and it had been a while since she'd had any. In front of her was a young woman, clearly eager to be in the hands of someone more experienced. How could she pass that up? Plus, her clit was on fire. Like an animal who smells food and suddenly realizes it's hungry, the area between her legs sensed the potential for sex and signaled her readiness.

Somehow, the two made it to Sara's bed, lying side by side, lost in one another's kisses. Sara's hand strayed from Dee's back and slid down her ass, pulling her in tight.

"Wanna be fucked by a woman?" Sara whispered in Dee's ear.

"Uh-huh," Dee said, her voice trembling slightly.

Sara wondered if Dee had ever been fucked, period, but didn't want to have that, or any, conversation. She rolled over on top of Dee, their legs intertwined, the heat of their groins feeding off one another.

Sara on top of her, the weight of her body, the pressure between her legs. It seemed almost too good to be real. As they kissed, Sara began rocking her hips, pressing her pelvis into Dee's.

"Mmm," moaned Dee. Without thinking, she moved in time with Sara and soon Dee felt a wetness between her legs as their bodies crashed into one another over and over. When Sara paused to undo the button on Dee's pants, Dee was only too eager to help. As a result, her pant legs became stuck on the ends of her legs. She struggled impatiently with her jeans.

"I got them." Sara got up and slid them off while glancing into Dee's eyes, searching for permission. She must have seen what she needed, for she reached forward and pulled Dee's underwear down. Dee lifted her hips to help.

Sara made quick work of her own clothes, stripping naked and throwing her clothes on the floor. Back on the bed, she leaned forward and pulled Dee's shirt up but couldn't remove it as Dee still lay on her back. Dee's face betrayed her nervousness, but she sat up nonetheless and pulled her shirt over her head. Sara reached around her and undid her bra, tossing it over her shoulder. With a hand, she nudged Dee back down onto the bed and followed, allowing their naked bodies to meet, breast to breast and groin to groin.

"Are you nervous?" Sara asked, having pushed up onto her elbows in order to see Dee's face.

Dee considered lying but found herself answering truthfully without realizing she'd chosen to. "Yeah. A little."

"We can stop if you want."

Dee shook her head.

"Now or at any time. You just say the word. Okay?"

Dee nodded.

Sara smiled and lowered her body back down onto Dee, kissing her on the mouth as she did so. Dee also stopped holding back. Her kisses became more intense, her tongue teasing Sara's as it craved something more, some place different. Sara broke off their kiss to kiss and lick Dee's nipple, finally latching onto her breast only when Dee's moans communicated her appreciation and longing for more.

Alternately sucking her breast and licking it, Sara moved from one side to the other, gauging Dee's response, before settling on her right breast as the most sensitive. Sara sucked faster, her body's excitement growing for what she hoped would come next. Her hand rubbed up and down Dee's leg, the top, the outside, the inside. Sara shifted, making room for her hand, which stroked Dee's folds, taking up her wetness, turned on by her groans.

Dee thought her body might explode. The area between her legs was hot and pulsing, pleasure craving more pleasure. With Sara's mouth on her breast and now her fingers between Dee's legs, stroking her wetness, she brought forth a level of pleasure Dee didn't know was possible. She wanted to stay like this forever.

Sara enjoyed stroking Dee, feeling her pleasure rise, and so would come back. But now she needed to fuck. Sliding easily in Dee's abundant juices, Sara's fingers circled Dee's opening and dipped over the edge, testing Dee's response. The soft moan was permission enough. Sara slid slowly, carefully, into Dee, her tightness suggesting tension or signaling that it was, indeed, her first time.

"You okay?" Sara asked.

"Mmm, yeah. There's a little pain, but it also feels amazing."

"Want me to keep going?"

"Yes," Dee said without hesitation, her voice conveying certainty.

With that permission, Sara pulled out slightly before pushing back in, moving on Dee, rocking gently with her whole body. Over and over, they came together, their bodies moving in unison. Sara's body moved in time with her hand, fucking Dee again and again.

Dee threw her arms around Sara's neck, the latter noting Dee's rapid, shallow breathing and also how she rocked her hips in time to Sara's thrusts.

"You good?" Sara asked. It was, after all, Dee's first time.

"Mmm."

Sara wanted to let go. Needed to let go. But it was Dee's first time. And while she wanted to fuck with abandon, and let in the heat building between her own legs control her, she restrained herself, or at least tried to. There were times it seemed if she could only get more of her body inside, her pleasure would spill out and she'd actually ejaculate. This was one of those times. But Sara held back from chasing a sensation that remained just out of reach. Perhaps another time.

"I ... I think I've had enough," Dee whispered.

"Oh, are you getting sore?" Sara asked.

"Yeah," Dee said sheepishly.

"It's nothing to be ashamed of." Sara pulled out. "It's to be expected, actually."

"But I didn't have an orgasm."

"Oh, but we're not done yet. I mean, unless you want to be."

Dee's face betrayed her confusion.

"Lots of women, straight women even, can't come just by being fucked. That's not how we get off. Lie back and relax. I'll stop, of course, if you want me to, but let's see if you don't like this."

Before Dee had time to answer, Sara had spread Dee's legs apart and disappeared between them. The second Sara's tongue touched Dee's sweet wetness, Dee let out a long moan. She'd never experienced anything that came even close to this. At that moment, her entire body, her whole being, consisted of the area between her legs, under Sara's tongue. Nothing else existed, nothing else mattered.

"Mmm," Sara responded, her tongue lazily exploring every inch between Dee's legs as if she had all the time in the world. She'd lick her clit, rub her tongue in circles upon it, and move off of it, her intention for Dee's pleasure to climb, but not too quickly.

Dee thought she'd lose her mind. The area under Sara's tongue was sending out wave upon wave of pleasure, but right when she was about to fall off the cliff and climax, Sara's tongue would move down into her folds, still feeling sensational, but keeping her away from the edge.

The next time Sara did this, Dee couldn't stand it any longer. So when Sara's tongue finally migrated up to her clit, Dee put her hand on Sara's head and held it there. The direct pressure had Dee moaning almost continuously, and as she neared climax, she cried out.

"Oh!... Oh!... Oh!" Each cry of Dee's grew higher in pitch until, finally, she let out an elongated cry, high yet soft. An

wasn't as if he didn't know if he'd read the journal. She'd written a lot about that night. How she felt being with the team at the barbecue, her conversation with Sara, and what followed.

"No daughter of mine is gay." Her dad's words came out as a whisper, but with venom and spite.

Dee stared at him. What was she supposed to say to that?

"Sweetie," her mother said, "we'd like to get you some help. Clearly you've been spending time with undesirable individuals."

Undesirable individuals? What the hell? Dee couldn't believe this was happening. A layer of judgment weighed down the air in the room, making it difficult for Dee to breathe. Instead of holding her head down in shame, she glanced from one parent to the other.

Then she exploded. "They're not undesirable individuals!" Her voice was loud, insistent and full of anger. All these years she put up with their vitriol, throwing slurs around as easily as if they were discussing the weather. Did she find the courage to speak out because she finally realized she was gay? Probably. But also, in this moment, she realized her teammates were becoming her friends. And while she rarely stood up for herself, she would take a stand for her friends.

"Do not use that tone with your mother." Her father's eyes flashed a warning, but Dee was finally beyond caring. "You've been lying to us, Daphne. Telling us you've been going to a study group when you were playing softball." He tried to stare her down, but for one of the first times in her life, she didn't drop her gaze.

The volume of her father's voice dropped, and he seemed to be trying to change tack. As if he could convince her he was just a caring father wanting what was best for her. His patronizing

31

tone made Dee want to scream.

"Now, there's someone we want you to see. He specializes in working with those who are confused about … Well, we think he can help you. You have an appointment with him tomorrow."

"Help me?" Dee said exasperatedly. "What do I need help with, exactly, father?"

"Making better choices, dear," her mother piped in.

"Choices, huh?" Dee shook her head. She was about to argue but had enough experience with that to realize it would be like banging her head against a brick wall. She'd get nowhere but have a gigantic headache. "Fine," she spat. "What's his name?" While she had no intention of seeing this person, she figured it was the only way to extricate herself from this conversation.

"Pastor Wallace—"

"Pastor Wallace?" she interrupted, incredulous. "Are you kidding me?" Her voice went up an octave. Dee had jumped up from the couch. "You've heard the rumors about him, haven't you?"

"What are you talking about, dear?" her mother asked. Her mom could be so clueless sometimes.

"He can't always keep his hands to himself."

"That's quite enough!" Her father's voice rang through the house. "I will not have you talking about Pastor Wallace like that. Now, go to your room."

Her father hadn't told her to go to her room since she'd been in high school, but she welcomed the excuse to escape the living room. She stormed upstairs and flopped onto her bed. She pulled out her phone, wanting a distraction from the rage and fear coursing inside her. Without realizing it, she searched for information on Pastor Wallace online, figuring it couldn't make her feel any worse. She was wrong.

According to her search, Pastor Wallace's counseling services centered on the practice of conversion therapy. While she remembered hearing of the term, she'd paid it no heed. Until now. The more research she did, the angrier and more scared she became. She needed to talk to someone. But who?

The only person on the team for whom she had contact information was Sara. Did she really want to reach out to her? And if she did, would Sara even talk to her? Well, she needed someone to turn to. It seemed too much for Dee to call her on the phone at that moment. A text she could manage.

Sara. It's Dee. I know I blew u off at practice, but I need help and don't know where else to turn. She pushed send.

Her phone pinged less than a minute later.

What's wrong?

My parents. They read my diary and want to send me to conversion therapy.

Her phone pinged again.

What do u need?

Footsteps came down the hall. Instinctively, Dee turned her phone to silent and clicked back to the web browser.

Chapter 6

"Are you texting with someone?" her father asked.

"Why? Is that illegal now?" Dee asked.

"I don't want you interacting with those teammates of yours anymore."

"Fine."

"Give me your phone."

"Why?"

"Just give it to me." Her dad bought her the phone and paid the bill, so she didn't really have a choice. She pushed the button on the side of the phone to restore the lock screen. She handed over the phone.

"What's your passcode?"

"I'm not giving you the passcode."

Her father glared at her, then turned and walked away. He stopped at the doorway and spoke over his shoulder, not looking back. "You're meeting with Pastor Wallace tomorrow at two o'clock. Your mother and I will be taking you to your appointment."

Dee didn't respond. Her father waited a moment before walking away. She sat on her bed, stunned, frozen, lost and scared. The two people who were supposed to protect her, love her unconditionally, had instead judged her and found not only fault but a sickness they found revolting. Their blindness, their unwillingness to not only accept her truth but ignore that of Pastor Wallace was not only callous and a betrayal, but dangerous. Sitting on her bed, staring at the floor, it finally came to her. What she needed to do.

Luckily, her parents weren't technologically savvy or aware of the various options for communication. She opened her computer, muted the volume, and opened her message app. There were multiple messages from Sara.

???

Are you okay?

I'm not mad at u for what happened at practice. I'm here if u need me.

My dad took my phone. I'm on my computer.

I was getting worried.

I'm worried. I can't stay here anymore. But I don't know what to do.

Footsteps came down the hall. Dee switched apps on her computer and a document appeared on the screen. At the last second, she remembered to turn off notifications for her messages.

This time, it was her mom. They did this often. Played tag team.

"What are you doing, sweetie?"

"Working on a paper for class."

"Oh, okay. Well, there's pie in the kitchen if you'd like some."

"Okay."

Her mom stared at her for a moment, her face a mixture of sadness and confusion. She said nothing else, but turned on her heel and retreated from the room.

Dee waited a moment before opening her messages.

U can stay with me.

Or I'm sure we can find somewhere else.

Sorry, my mom came to check on me. I don't know what to do. If I leave, I don't think I can ever come back.

U don't know that. But can u afford to stay?

Dee stared at that last line. Could she afford to stay? Now that she understood and owned her truth? No. But she didn't have much money. She worked fifteen hours a week, earning minimum wage. What would she do? The only thing she was confident of was the fact that there was no way she was getting into a room with Pastor Wallace.

I'm stuck here. I have no money or ...

Some things are more important than that. But I'll support u whatever u decide.

If she left, her parents were sure to cut her off. She only worked a few hours at her job.

But you can get more, a voice in her head said.

But will it be enough?

You'll figure it out.

Movement on her screen caught her eye. Sara sent another text.

I checked in with others on the team. Several people said they have extra rooms.

Scared and overwhelmed, Dee stared at the screen. If she listened to her gut, she realized she didn't have a choice. She had to go. But it would be better if she made a plan. What did she need? Clothes, her computer. She'd need to get her phone. And some money. Her parents always kept some cash on hand. If they despised her for being gay, taking money wouldn't make it worse. For them, there was nothing worse than being gay.

Thank goodness she'd paid for the car with her own money.

At least they couldn't report the car stolen, something she wouldn't put past them. Staring out the bedroom window but seeing nothing in the darkness, she made up her mind.

Can I come tonight?

Absolutely.

I need to wait until my parents are asleep. I need to find my phone and some other stuff.

Ok. Come anytime. Let me know if u need anything.

Thanks

Dee glanced around her room, taking a visual inventory before making a list of everything she wanted to bring. She shouldn't start packing until her parents went to bed, which was usually around ten o'clock. Things like her school books, computer and phone charger she put in her backpack as that wouldn't raise suspicion. And while she didn't think her stomach could handle pie, or to be around her parents, she wanted to locate her phone and her dad's wallet. So she left her room and joined her parents in the kitchen.

"There's my sweet girl," her mom said, a statement that often grated on Dee but now was simply nauseating. Her dad sat on the couch in the living room watching T.V.

Dee managed a weak, but hopefully convincing, smile. As her mom served her pie, Dee spotted her phone on the kitchen counter. Her car keys hung on the hook, as usual. She didn't see her dad's wallet. That was okay, though. They always kept an emergency stash of money in a coffee can under the sink, and she should be able to take some without them noticing. Dee did her best to down the pie, though she didn't taste a bite.

After complaining of being tired, she said goodnight and retreated to her bedroom. While anxiety had her itching to pack her bags, a gut feeling told her not to. Instead, she brushed her teeth and changed for bed as usual, which proved to be a wise decision. Her dad came down the hall to check on her one last time, and luckily, she lay in bed. Light from the hallway told Dee he'd pushed open the door, but she stayed still with her back to the door.

Fifteen minutes later, when it seemed certain neither of her parents would wander back down to her room, she got out of bed. The full moon cast enough light that she didn't need to turn on her lamp. Ten minutes later, two duffle bags of clothes plus her backpack of books, computer and charger were ready to go. She tiptoed down the hallway to the bathroom, and before retrieving some necessities, continued past to make sure the rest of the house was dark.

Once she'd packed her toiletries, she carried everything back down the hall to the kitchen. Rolls of twenty-dollar bills filled the coffee can under the kitchen. Her parents probably knew exactly how much money they kept here. Would they call the police on her? This crossed her mind as she reached into the can. Her parents would be mad as hell when they found out she left. That they read her diary and wanted her to speak with Pastor Wallace made her wonder if they wouldn't turn her in. She covered the can without taking a single bill, but then froze with her hand on the plastic cover. With only five dollars in her wallet, she needed more money. Opening the can, she removed two bills, enough to help her, but not enough for them to be certain she'd taken any. She hoped.

With her phone in her pocket and keys in hand, she turned to leave and saw her diary on the table in the living room. She grabbed it on her way out, slipping out the front door with barely a sound. Once in the car, she backed out of the driveway. As she pulled away, a light in her parents' bedroom window, which faced the driveway, flicked on. Dee drove away, tears in her eyes.

She knocked on Sara's door twenty minutes later.

Sara opened it. "Hey, Dee. Come on in."

At the sight of her teammate, Dee finally broke down. She stood on the doorstep, tears running down her face, her body shaking. The adrenaline that had fueled her became overpowered by underlying stress and bewilderment.

Without a word, Sara stepped forward, wrapped her in a hug and held her there on the doorstep, letting her unload some of her grief and confusion.

"Let's get you inside," Sara said a minute or two later, when Dee seemed more in control.

Sara grabbed Dee's bags and led her into the house. For the next hour, they sat at a table off the kitchen. Sara listened while Dee talked. She recited the evening's events in detail, needing someone else to know everything about what had happened.

"Shit. My parents are going to be pissed." Dee held her head in her hands. "Was I stupid to leave?" She glanced up. "I was stupid to leave, wasn't I? Oh. What am I going to do?"

"Dee. They were going to send you to conversion therapy with a pedophile. I think you made the right decision."

Dee glanced at Sara, her eyes narrowed. "They were, weren't they?"

"I've set up the couch for you for tonight. We can talk in the morning about what to do next. Rose and her girlfriend offered their spare room. So did Mannie and her partner."

"Okay. And Sara. Thank you so much. I don't know what I would have done."

"Don't worry about it. Try and get some sleep, okay?"

Dee nodded and watched Sara slip into her bedroom.

Ten minutes later, Dee stood in the doorway to Sara's room. Sara sat up in bed. "Is everything okay?"

"Can I sleep in here?" Dee asked. "Just for tonight? I don't really want to be alone."

Without a second thought, Sara scooted over in bed. "Sure. You'll need to grab the pillow off the couch."

Dee slipped into bed next to Sara and lay flat on her back, staring at the ceiling. While she hadn't wanted to be alone, now that she was in Sara's bed, an awkward self-consciousness threatened to envelop her. Exhaustion eventually saved her from her feelings of unease, and she fell asleep wondering what the next day would bring.

The sound of running water awakened her. Five minutes later, Sara came into the bedroom, dressed. "How are you this morning?"

"I'm not sure."

"Well, I hate to run out on you like this, but I have to go to work. Help yourself to anything. I mean that. There's food in the fridge, and feel free to go through the cupboards. I suspect you'll find something you'd like to eat. I'll be back around five-thirty. We can talk more then, okay?"

Dee nodded.

"You sure you'll be alright?"

"I'll manage." She didn't tell Sara that she had class that day and had no intention of attending. But once Sara left, and Dee had eaten, she realized she could do with a distraction. So she drove to school and stopped by her job at the supermarket to inquire about getting more hours.

Chapter 7

That night, having procured extra hours at work, Dee was feeling better, if only a little. True, she'd ignored five phone calls from her parents and was too scared to listen to her voicemail. But she now had thirty hours at work, up from fifteen, and she could still make her classes at the community college. There wouldn't be time for much else, but she'd be able to go to at least one of her softball practices, and she'd volunteered to work every Sunday to avoid working every other Saturday.

Dee took the initiative and made dinner, wanting to chip in and hoping Sara wouldn't mind.

Sara walked in as Dee was adding minced garlic to sauteed onions in a pan on the stove. "Oh! Something smells good! I might need to keep you around if you're going to cook."

Dee smiled, suddenly shy. She finished cooking up the chicken stir-fry while Sara changed.

"What did you end up doing today?" Sara said, as she walked out of her bedroom, pulling a shirt over her head.

"Went to class and stopped by work to talk to my boss. I was able to get more hours at work, which is a relief."

"That's great," Sara said. She poured herself some ice tea from the fridge. "Do you need any help?"

"No. I'm good."

While Dee finished cooking, Sara read through her mail, both physical letters and email. She waited until dinner to pepper Dee with more questions. Toward the end of dinner, Dee mentioned the issue with her voicemail.

Sara interrupted her. "Can I see your phone?"

"Sure."

"Unlock it for me."

Dee wasn't sure what Sara was doing, but did as she asked.

Sara put the phone to her ear, listened before hitting the delete button and repeated this several times before handing the phone back to Dee. "There. No more voicemails."

"But what if there was something important?"

"There wasn't. But that's why I listened. Nothing they said would have been good for you to hear. I promise."

"Thanks. I think." Dee said this with a mixture of dread and relief. "But what did they say?" She figured it was too much to hope that they'd apologized. She was right.

"I don't think you would gain anything by listening to them. Really. Your dad started out mad, then conciliatory, then really pissed off, and your mom pleaded."

"Pleaded? Pleaded for what?"

"For you to come home and go see Pastor whatever his name is."

"Pastor Wallace," Dee said automatically. She suddenly had the urge to clear the air from before. "I never really apologized for blowing you off at softball practice."

"It's okay." Sara took a drink of ice water. "And I shouldn't have let things go as far as they did that night."

"Do you regret it?" Dee asked. She took a drink of water,

needing something to do with her hands. They'd both finished eating.

"No. Not at all. And I'd do it again … Um, forget I said that." Sara paused, the air now filled with a new energy, an electric charge that pulsed around and between them. Sara plowed on. "I meant what I said about not wanting a relationship with you. No offense. But I'm not willing to be someone's first love again. I did it before, and I promised myself I wouldn't do it again."

"What happened?"

"I'd rather not go into it. But give yourself some time. I mean, you just came out. You can count the time you've been out in hours. Okay," Sara smiled, "well maybe you're up to days, but you know what I mean."

Dee smiled. "I do. So … Should I see if I can stay with Mannie or Rose?"

"You can if you want. But you're welcome to stay here a while if you'd like."

Dee got the impression that Sara was purposefully not looking at her.

"Can I stay another night or two?"

"Of course." Sara grabbed both their plates and got up from the table. "But don't feel like you have to cook dinner."

"I don't mind. But I'm working tomorrow night, so I won't be here until late."

That night, they decided to watch a movie together on the couch, though they sat at opposite ends. As Sara scrolled through the options, Dee blurted out without thinking, "I don't regret it either."

"What?… Oh." Sara glanced at Dee. "But you may."

"What makes you say that?"

"Those puppy-dog eyes, for one."

At those words, Dee blushed and looked away.

"Hey," Sara said, reaching for Dee's arm. "I didn't say that to make you feel bad or embarrass you. Dee. I'm sorry. I should have realized it might."

Dee nodded.

"Dee. We've all been there. It's okay. Dee, look at me."

With difficulty, Dee met Sara's gaze. Then her eyes dropped to Sara's lips. Dee couldn't help herself. She'd had a thing for Sara from the moment they met, though she didn't recognize her feelings for what they were.

Sara didn't come closer. But neither did she move away. She was immobilized by the voices in her head, holding a disciplinary meeting and talking over one another.

"Shit!" Sara said to herself, though, of course, Dee heard her. "You'll need to watch the movie without me. Sorry." Sara got up and left the room, closing the door to her bedroom after her.

Dee sat on the couch feeling stupid and a fool. More to distract herself than from any real desire to watch anything, she scrolled through the movie directory. Once the movie started, she found herself not paying attention. A growing warmth emanating from between her legs joined the voices in her head to block out the scenes in the make-believe universe on the screen in front of her.

Something else seemed to take control of Dee's body, for somehow she was standing in front of Sara's bedroom door, but she didn't remember getting up from the couch. She knocked softly on the door.

"Come in."

Sara was sitting up in bed, a loose tank top barely covering her chest. She seemed to expect Dee to come knocking. The two women stared at one another. "I don't want to be your girlfriend."

"I know."

"Do you? Right now, you're being ruled by what's between your legs. But how will you feel tomorrow? Last time you got your feelings hurt and wouldn't talk to me. Remember?"

"How will you feel tomorrow?" Dee threw the question back at her. "Are you telling me you have no feelings for me at all?"

Sara didn't answer, because she didn't know what to say. Three years ago, she'd been Rebecca's first love, and after ten months, they'd parted less than amicably. Was it that? And did their bitter parting have anything to do with it being Rebecca's first lesbian relationship or something else? Since then, Sara had plenty of one-night stands, but nothing that could be called a relationship or even dating. A quiet voice in her head wondered if there was something about that parting that she hadn't dealt with yet. She pushed it aside. Now was not the time for processing. When is it ever a good time for processing?

"I don't want a relationship," Sara said.

"But you want to sleep with me," Dee said.

"I want to sleep with a lot of women," Sara countered. "And I do," she added.

"You do sleep with other women or you do want to sleep with me?" Dee asked.

Sara opened her mouth to speak but closed it again, choosing not to reply.

Dee stood in the middle of the room, and the two women stared at each other. She was nineteen years old. But at this moment, she might as well have been closer to fifteen. Hormones scrambled the connection to her rational brain. Her clit was on fire and controlled her actions now. Sara had the capacity to make responsible, conscious decisions. She realized and understood the ramifications of any decision she made. She just didn't care. Throwing the covers off her legs revealed she wasn't wearing any pants, her way of providing Dee with an invitation. Take it or leave it.

Dee closed the gap, climbing on top of the bed and sitting on Sara, straddling her. Without a word, she looked into Sara's eyes. Sara placed a hand on the back of Dee's head and pulled her down, kissing her hard on the lips. They sucked each other's lips, let their tongues collide and explored each other's mouths. Within seconds, Dee's hands found Sara's breasts, alternately rubbing the tops of her nipples with her thumbs and grasping the firm yet soft flesh.

Sara turned them over and slid down, so Dee lay on her back on the bed. She relieved Dee of her clothes, removing her own underwear too. Her hand immediately dove between Dee's legs, her fingers dancing in her folds. As her fingers touched Dee's abundant wetness, Sara's own desire surged. Despite what she told herself, Sara wanted to be back inside of Dee again. At night, when she lay in bed by herself, she'd remember them fucking, and masturbate. She told herself it was only because Dee was the last woman she'd fucked, but her gut, which she'd ignored until now, suggested otherwise.

"Ooh!" Only after she'd moaned did Sara realize she'd done so. Plunging into Dee, feeling her wetness surrounding her finger, taking her in, was almost more than she could handle. But she hadn't wanted Dee to know how good it was for her.

Sara moved on Dee, fucking in a rhythm that Dee followed. Together they moved as if dancing, with neither stepping on the other's feet. Dee's arms wrapped around Sara's shoulders, holding her tight, her hips rocking in sync with Sara's.

"It's so good," Dee said, the first of the two to speak since Dee approached the bed.

"Uh ... uh," Sara groaned as she thrust into Dee. "It is," she said, forgetting herself and her promise to stay detached. Over and over, they moved together, finding pleasure in each other's body. Sara wondered if this time Dee would get sore, but Dee showed no sign of wanting to stop.

Dee released one hand from Sara's back and reached down between her legs.

No, Sara thought. She paused, deep inside of Dee. "You don't have to do that. I can go down on you again and still be inside you."

"I want to," Dee said. "I want to feel your body on me, inside me, when I come."

A note of panic sparked out from Sara's core, threatening to blossom, to take over the moment. Her mind traveled backwards, against her best intentions. Her relationship with Rebecca fell apart when Rebecca didn't need Sara anymore. Once Rebecca developed confidence in herself sexually, once she'd become comfortable being out, she'd shed Sara like an outgrown holey sweater. It left Sara with nothing but a sense of being used. And she'd never quite recovered.

In the time it took Sara to reminisce, Dee's hand moved between their bodies and her moans became more consistent, not to mention louder. She seemed less inhibited than only a week ago.

"Don't stop," Dee said, her voice sounding a command, before adding, "please," which sounded more wishful and pleading.

Sara struggled but successfully shut her mind, or at least enough to proceed. Again she moved, thrusting, plunging, fucking, this time with renewed vigor. Her movements were more intense, her penetration deeper, harder. Luckily, Dee got off on it and didn't recognize that there might be more to Sara's fucks than just fucking. Was Sara chasing after something, or running away? Either way, she had to go faster. She just had to.

"Ahh!... Ahh...! Oh, don't stop! Ahh!... Ah!... Ahhhh!" Dee's body tightened around Sara as she screamed out and climaxed. Sara didn't stop fucking her as she came, continuing until Dee put her hand on hers. "Sara. Sara, stop. Come out."

Sara stopped, pulled out, and collapsed onto Dee, trying to hide the silent tears sliding down her cheeks. As she lay there, unable to control the flow of tears, Sara hoped Dee would assume she was just allowing her to recover.

"Oh, that was amazing," Dee said several moments later.

"Umm," Sara said convincingly.

"You know," Dee said, "I think it's your turn." She pushed up, intending to roll Sara off of her.

"Not now. I'm good." Sara said, not ready to face Dee.

"What do you mean? Hey, look at me." Dee couldn't see Sara's face with her turned away. Sara didn't move. With strength Sara didn't know she had, Dee pushed her up and off, sitting on top of her, her legs folded underneath and on either side of Sara.

"What if I want to—" Dee's voice was playful but cut off when she glimpsed Sara's face. "What's wrong?"

Chapter 8

Sara wiped her eyes with the sheet like one would wipe at newly spilled catsup. "I'm fine."

"Fine? You don't seem fine."

"Well, I am. Now, can I get up?" Sara made to sit up.

"Absolutely not." Dee pushed her down, one hand on each of her shoulders, her face inches from Sara's. "Tell me what's going on. Did I do—?"

"Not everything's about you, Dee." The words came out mean, nasty even. Definitely dismissive.

Hurt, Dee rolled off Sara, grabbed her clothes and walked out of the bedroom, slamming the door behind her.

Dee dressed, so angry and confused she tripped while trying to put her underwear on while standing and fell onto the couch. This only made her more pissed off. She didn't want to stay, but she couldn't leave. It was late and calling one of her other teammates and asking to stay on such short notice seemed melodramatic. But she'd leave tomorrow. First thing.

With the lights off, Dee settled onto the couch, knowing she wouldn't be able to sleep. At the sound of Sara's door opening, Dee rolled over and placed her back to Sara's room, hoping

Sara would think Dee was asleep.

No such luck.

The end of the couch where Dee rested her legs sank down several inches. Dee didn't move.

"Her name was Rebecca." Sara's voice sounded as if each word cost her dearly. "She was younger than me by three or four years, and as she struggled to come out, she latched onto me like a lost child to her mother. Therapy would probably have been the best place for her, but she talked to me instead. And I listened as best I could and offered support. But then it turned into more. We slept together once or twice, and then we became a thing. We kind've fell into being girlfriends. Things were good for a while. But as her confidence grew, and she needed me less, she seemed less interested in having me as a girlfriend. And one day she walked out of my apartment and never came back. Hooked up with someone else almost immediately."

The hum of the refrigerator thirty feet away filled the silence. Dee rolled over to her other side, propping her head on her hand, her elbow sinking into the couch.

"I don't want to go through that again," Sara said.

"I'm not her."

"You could be."

"But I'm not. Was she a blonde?"

"No," Sara chuckled, despite herself. "Definitely not."

"See. Not the same person." Dee sat up and sat next to Sara. Their shoulders touched. "Did she have long hair?"

Sara smirked. "Kind of. Almost as long as yours."

"Well, I've wanted to cut it for a long time."

"Don't do it on my account. It wouldn't change anything."

"No, I suppose it wouldn't," Dee said. "I'm sorry Rebecca broke your heart, Sara. I really am. And maybe you don't want a relationship right now. And maybe I shouldn't be in one either. Who knows? Just don't make me out to be someone I'm not."

They sat in silence for a moment. And then, because she couldn't handle her growing discomfort in the silence, and also because it was on her mind, she returned to the issue of her hair.

"Did you know that the only thing that's kept me from cutting my hair is my parents? I've talked about cutting it for years." Dee smacked herself on the forehead. "I'm so stupid sometimes."

"What?"

"They probably didn't want me to cut my hair cause they were afraid I'd look less feminine."

"Or more dykish," Sara added.

"Exactly. Which is why I think you should cut it for me."

Sara stared disbelievingly at Dee. "When?"

"Now." A smile stretched its way across Dee's face. That she could actually cut her hair made her so happy. Having it cut would be a greater act of defiance. No, it wasn't to get back at her parents. An act of expressing herself, perhaps, almost equal to her announcing that she was gay.

"Now?" Sara said incredulously.

"Why not?"

"Because I don't know a thing about cutting hair."

Dee got up and walked to the kitchen, coming back with scissors. She held them out to Sara.

"You want me to cut your hair at eleven o'clock at night?"

"Uh-huh. And then I want to—"

"Do you have to work tomorrow?" cut in Sara.

"Yep. But not until the afternoon."

"So you can go get it fixed if you need to?"

"Yep. And then I want to—"

51

"Do you promise to get it cut properly tomorrow?"

"If I don't like what you've done? Yes."

Sara didn't respond except to hold out her hand. She paused. "You sure we aren't drunk and doing something stupid?"

"Pretty sure. This hair hasn't fit me for a long time. And now that I've realized I can get it cut, I don't want to wait another minute. You'd be doing me a favor."

"You're not going to stop talking to me if I butcher it?"

"Nope. I might not talk to you for other reasons," Dee said playfully.

"Well, come into the bathroom where there's more light and a garbage can."

Once out of its ponytail, Dee's hair lay across her mid-back. "Cut it here." Dee put her fingers an inch above her shoulders.

"You sure?"

"Yep."

"How about I cut it a little longer to start? Yep. I'll do that."

Dee didn't say anything, afraid if she did Sara might back out. But Sara held the scissors to Dee's hair and made the first cut.

"No going back now." Three more cuts and Sara stepped back. "How's that?" She asked Dee, who stood gazing fixedly in the mirror.

"Well, it's not the straightest..." Her voice was serious, but her eyes danced in the mirror.

"What?"

"Just kidding." Dee shook her head. "It's so much lighter. Freer. I feel freer." She looked at Sara in the mirror. "Thanks. I mean, I will make that appointment tomorrow, but thanks." She smiled. "And you didn't let me finish what I was going to say before."

"Oh, I didn't?"

"Nope. After you asked if I wanted you to cut my hair at eleven o'clock at night, I said, 'Yes, and then I want to,' and you cut me off." Dee turned to face Sara. "What I was going to say was, and then I want to fuck you." Dee surprised herself with her boldness. But she was on a roll. No reason to stop now.

Sara opened her mouth and closed it again. Her time of feeling sad and protective of her heart had passed, at least for that moment. And despite her nearly butchering Dee's hair, Dee looked good with shorter hair. Quite good, in fact.

"But do you know how?" Sara quipped.

Dee turned around, faced Sara, and walked toward her. Sara walked backward, keeping some distance between the two of them. Her eyes twinkled. "Short hair suits you. A much better look, I'd say."

"Why, thank you," Dee said, still advancing on Sara. She lunged at Sara, grabbed her, and held her tight. Their eyes met, each searching the other's. Silently they came to an understanding of sorts, leaned in and kissed, a soft, sweet, tender kiss. Their embrace quickly intensified, their hands groping, holding, grasping. Somehow, they made it into the bedroom. Clothes flew off and Dee sat on Sara's stomach, straddling her.

"So, did you want to give me a step-by-step lesson on how to fuck you, or may I proceed on my own?"

"I cut your hair off and suddenly you're a smartass?"

"Guess so."

Dee leaned over and kissed Sara before sitting up again. Staring into Sara's eyes, Dee slipped her hand down between Sara's legs and moved within her folds.

"Ooh, someone's wet," Dee said.

She rubbed Sara's clit until Sara could no longer maintain eye contact, closing her eyes to the pleasure. Dee took that moment to slide her fingers down to her opening and plunge inside.

Caught off guard, Sara's eyes popped open. Dee smiled at her and thrust her hand in and out, fucking her hard and fast. "How's that?" Dee paused deep inside, moving her finger around.

"Mmm," Sara said.

Dee continued fucking Sara, demonstrating skills she didn't even realize she had. But she wanted more. She withdrew from Sara, repositioned herself between Sara's legs—after playfully pushing her legs apart with her hands—and settled down between them. Dee gazed at Sara's pussy, never having seen another's up close. With her fingers, she explored her folds and her clit, her fingers sliding softly in her wetness. She leaned in and licked her, tasting sweetness on her tongue.

Sara moaned at the first touch of Dee's tongue to her folds, which encouraged Dee. Dee remembered how amazing it was when someone went down on her. Now she would return the favor. She didn't have to think about what to do. She was a woman, after all. Her tongue made a zigzag route from Sara's opening up to her clit and back down again, eliciting another moan.

That Sara expressed such pleasure was all Dee needed. Her mouth sank into Sara, her tongue dancing and exploring, her lips kissing and sucking. Sara's moans became louder and more consistent. Finally, Dee zeroed in on her clit, licking it side to side and round and round. She pressed down on it, sucking it, enjoying the sensation of it swelling in her mouth.

With one particular movement, a circular licking with a slight downward pressure, Sara rose toward climax.

It took moments with Dee between her legs before Sara

relaxed and got out of her head. A voice kept telling her in so many ways to not let go, to not let her guard down. That if she came, it might mean something. It might suggest she had feelings for Dee. But Sara argued with herself. Having an orgasm didn't mean she had feelings for Dee. This wasn't her first one-night stand. And they'd never meant anything before. Then why was this different? If she had feelings for Dee, it was because she had feelings for Dee. Oh shit!

The awareness of her feelings for the woman currently between her legs, who felt amazing despite it being the first time going down on a woman, broke through Sara's resistance.

"Oh, don't stop!" she cried.

"Mmm," Dee moaned.

It was hard for Dee not to speed up or change her pressure, for as Sara's moans and cries intensified, Dee's inclination was to do one of those things to help her come. But Sara asked her not to stop, which probably meant she wanted things to be kept the same. Dee did her best to contain her own excitement.

"Ahh!…Ahh!…Mmm."

Something changed in the tone of Sara's cries, and Dee noticed. They seemed more free somehow. Dee's tongue moved faster, pressing a little harder. This turned out to be exactly what Sara needed to come.

Her back arching, Sara cried out as her clit exploded with pleasure, shooting sparks, if such a thing were possible, down her legs and up her chest. Dee stayed, her tongue moving on Sara's clit, until Sara's hand pushed her away. Dee came up and onto Sara, holding her as her body rocked and rode the waves of orgasm.

With her mind blissfully quiet, Sara dozed off to sleep with Dee lying next to her.

Chapter 9

When Sara woke to her alarm the next morning, it took her half a second to remember what had happened the night before and why Dee was in her bed. Sara slipped out of the room without waking Dee and made herself a cup of coffee in the kitchen. She tried to evaluate how she really felt. Where were all her misgivings and boundaries she'd erected to prevent something like this from happening? Despite searching, despite asking herself a million questions and reminding herself of how Rebecca had broken her heart, she couldn't shake the light sensation in the middle of her chest.

"Maybe it's okay," she said to herself.

"Maybe what's okay?" Dee walked into the room unnoticed by Sara, who stood with her back to the entranceway.

"Huh?" Sara turned around. She hadn't realized she'd spoken out loud.

"I asked, what's okay?" Dee said, watching her but standing slightly off to the side. "You just said, 'Maybe it's okay,' and I was curious."

Sara shook her head but smiled. "Nothing. I didn't even realize I said anything. Want some coffee? I made a pot."

It was an obvious pivot, but Dee let it slide. After all, Sara seemed in a good mood and after last night, Dee wasn't sure what to expect. From either of them.

"Sure."

Sara grabbed her a mug, poured Dee a cup and handed it to her. "Thanks." Dee eyed her curiously. "I could have gotten it myself, you know."

Sara shrugged.

Dee spotted the sugar on the countertop and added a spoonful to her coffee. The two stood in the kitchen, drinking their coffee, silently stealing glances at one another.

Finally, Sara broke the silence. "You're working today, right?"

"Yeah, but not until three. I need to find somewhere to get my hair cut properly ... not," she grinned, "that you didn't do a marvelous job. How's it look, by the way? I haven't found a mirror yet."

"It actually isn't bad. There's one spot that's pretty uneven. If you can't get an appointment today, I'd be happy to do what I can to fix it."

"Let me try for an appointment first."

"Any regrets?"

"Nope. None." Dee shook her head from side to side. "I love how light it is." She took another sip from her mug. "Since I'm working tonight, can I stay here? I'll check with Mannie or Rose, probably Rose, to see if I can stay there until I figure out what I'm going to do."

"You can stay here." Sara spoke quietly, her cup to her lips, before taking a sip.

"Thanks, but there isn't an extra room, and I realized when I woke up this morning that it would be too hard for me."

"What would be too hard?" Sara asked.

"To be on the couch with you in the next room. I realize I

do have feelings for you, but ..." Dee put up her hand to stop Sara from interrupting her. "But, I'll be okay. I just think I need a little space." She gave a smile tinged with sadness. "Don't worry," she added, "I'll still talk to you at practice."

"I don't want you to take space," Sara said, her words so soft they came out as a whisper.

Dee's face was a canvas of confusion.

"I'm sorry for sounding so abrupt before," Sara said. "I'm so scared of getting burned again. But that could happen with anyone, regardless of if it's their first relationship or seventh."

"Seventh?"

"I don't know. I just picked a number. And don't interrupt."

Dee pulled her fingers across her lips, the hint of a smile on her face.

"I guess what I'm trying to say ..." Sara took a deep breath, "is that I want you to stay."

Dee gave her a look that clearly said, "Go on."

"I like you, Dee."

Dee continued to give her a look.

"I like you, and I'd like to see where this goes. This thing that you and I have started."

"This thing?"

"Damn. You gonna make me work for it?"

"Uh-huh." Dee smiled playfully.

Sara put her coffee mug down on the counter. Dee took a sip from hers, eyeing Sara over the rim. After Dee took her sip, Sara took her mug and placed it on the counter before wrapping her arms around her.

"Dee ... What's your last name?"

"Jones."

"Dee Jones. I would like you to stay here. In my house. With me. Until you find your own place, if you decide that's what you want. And I'd like to explore a relationship with you."

"You wanna be my girlfriend?"

Sara shook her head, causing the confused expression to appear on Dee's face again.

"I want you to be my girlfriend," Sara said with a straight face.

It took Dee a second, but then she slapped Sara on the ass.

"Is that a yes?" Sara quipped.

"Under one condition," Dee said seriously.

"What?" A hint of concern flashed across Sara's face.

"Never, under any circumstances ..." Dee paused, enjoying the look of consternation on Sara's face. "...take my coffee cup out of my hands."

Sara broke out into a smile. "You had me there for a second."

"I know I did."

"I think I need to get you back for that."

"Oh, really?" Dee said, breaking out of Sara's embrace and backing up.

"Really," Sara said, chasing Dee into the bedroom.

Chapter 10

Dee worked late Thursday night and arrived back at Sara's after midnight. She did her best to be quiet and felt lost, standing in the unfamiliar kitchen. For the first time since leaving home—Was it only two nights ago?—she missed her own space. Not that she wanted to go back to her parents. She didn't. But this felt like wearing a borrowed sweater that didn't quite fit right. It may be beautiful, but that didn't mean it was right for her. But she was about to slip into bed with a woman she'd been eyeing even before she realized she was gay. I must just be tired.

Dee pushed back her other thoughts and doubts, regarding her new haircut in the mirror as she brushed her teeth. She couldn't help but smile. On tiptoe, she approached the bed and slid in next to Sara, not wanting to wake her. While successful, Dee lay on her back, wondering how her life had changed so quickly. And why did it seem as if things were beyond her control?

By the time Dee woke up, Sara was gone. Dee sat at the table and ate breakfast, staring at her surroundings as if searching for something familiar before she showered and left for class.

After school, she grabbed a bite to eat before heading to her job.

The parking lot was full, and she didn't see the white Toyota Camry in the parking lot. Otherwise, she might have been able to prepare herself. But perhaps not.

She was through the parking lot and approaching the front of the building when she stopped in her tracks.

"Mom! What are you doing here?" Dee's mom sat on a bench outside the store, clearly waiting for Dee. "How'd you know I'd be working now?"

Her mom stood up from the bench, standing ramrod straight, her hands twisting in front of her. Mother and daughter remained ten feet apart. "I called and asked when you were scheduled to work next."

"Is Dad …?" Dee's voice trailed off as she glanced around, expecting her dad to walk up any second.

"He's not here. It's just me."

An awkward silence fell.

"You cut your hair."

Dee didn't answer. That she cut her hair was more than a little obvious. She knew her mother had more to say.

"You had such beautiful hair."

And there it was. "I have to get to work."

"Yes, of course, dear. Are you okay? Do you have someplace to stay?"

The idea of telling her mom that she was staying with her girlfriend crossed her mind, but she didn't want to sound spiteful. So she said, "Yes," while nodding.

Her mom reached out her hand. Dee took it. Her mom grasped it with her other hand, slipping a piece of paper to Dee. "I love you."

"I know, Mom. I've gotta go." Dee withdrew her hand and

61

walked away from her mom and into the store. Only when she got inside did she realize the paper her mom slipped into her hand was a one-hundred-dollar bill.

Like the night before, Dee didn't get back to Sara's until after midnight. Dee thought Sara might be up as it was Friday night, and it looked as if she had tried. She was asleep on the couch with the television on. Not sure whether to wake her, Dee did her best to be quiet as she walked through the house.

"Hey. Were you not going to wake me up?" Sara said drowsily from the couch.

Tiptoeing through the kitchen, Dee stopped and turned around. "I wasn't sure." She walked back toward the living room.

"You weren't sure?" Sara sat up, swinging her legs over the edge of the couch. "I didn't get to see you at all yesterday."

"I know. I just ..." Dee's voice trailed off. Conflicted, confused and disoriented, she dropped her gaze.

"Hey. What's up?" Sara considered asking Dee to join her on the couch but decided against it, getting up instead and wrapping her in a hug.

They stood facing one another. Sara's hands clasped around Dee's waist. She leaned back so she could see Dee's eyes.

"I ...," Dee started hesitantly. "It feels weird being here. It's your place, not mine."

"I didn't even think about how that might be hard for you. I'm sorry. How about we figure out ways to make it feel like yours, too?"

"Maybe." Dee didn't want to disappoint Sara. And perhaps this was just what lesbians did. "Okay, sure." She smiled, though still not convinced.

Sara leaned forward and kissed Dee on the lips. Dee kissed

her back and some of her confusion and worry melted away.

"How about we work on it tomorrow after the game?" Sara suggested.

"Oh right. I forgot about the game. How was practice yesterday?"

"Good. People asked about you."

"Did you tell them about us?"

"No," Sara said sheepishly.

"Why not?"

"They'd just give me a hard time."

"Why?"

Sara shrugged. "They just would." After a pause, she added, "You look tired."

The change of subject wasn't lost on Dee but tired as she was, she let it pass. "Yeah. It's been a long day."

Once in bed, Sara spooned Dee, and the latter relaxed into the embrace. Perhaps she was simply tired.

Dee awakened in the morning to the sensation of Sara's lips gently kissing her back and shoulder.

"Mmm." The sense of being out of place from the night before disappeared with whatever dreams she'd dreamt.

Dee rolled over on her back, and Sara climbed on top of her.

"Oh," Dee said, putting her hand over her mouth. "Morning breath."

"So don't kiss me," Sara said, taking Dee's nipple in her mouth and sucking.

"Mmm," Dee said. "But you're on my bladder and now I have to pee."

"Thwarted at the last second," Sara said, rolling off Dee.

When Dee got out of the bathroom, Sara was making coffee. Dee came up behind Sara and wrapped her arms around her.

"Can we go back to bed after coffee?"

"Did you forget?"

"What?"

"Our game is at nine thirty."

"Oh! I did. What time is it?"

"Eight. We're supposed to be there at nine. How about a rain check after the game?" Sara said.

"Sure," Dee smiled.

At their softball game, the team was quick to give Sara a hard time after they realized that she and Dee were together. While the two tried to keep it a secret—they'd decided to not tell the team yet—Mannie caught them glancing at one another the way new lovers do.

"You couldn't stay away, could you?" Mannie said to Sara as they walked out onto the field.

Sara smiled sheepishly.

"Is she moving in with you?" Mannie asked.

Sara nodded.

Mannie stopped midstep and stared at Sara. "Seriously?" If her facial expression didn't express her incredulity, her tone certainly did.

"What?" Sara's pretense at cluelessness didn't fool Mannie for a second. "She needed a place to stay.

Mannie approached Sara and put an arm around her shoulder, steering her toward right field.

"I won't let it affect the team," Sara said, trying to preempt the comments she knew were coming.

"You can't make that promise and you know it. But it's not just that. It must be a really vulnerable time for Dee right now. I just don't like the idea that you may be taking advantage of her."

"What!" Sara stopped suddenly and slipped out from under Mannie's arm. "What about what I want? Don't I get to have someone in my life?" Sara spoke louder than she'd intended and glanced over her shoulder to see if anyone had noticed.

They had.

Players from both teams were looking toward Sara and Mannie. That might also have been because a batter was standing right outside the batter's box, ready to hit. Sara glared at Mannie before running out to her position. Mannie hustled over to first base.

After the third out, when the team was in the dugout, Dee sidled up next to Sara. "What was that about?"

"Did everyone hear our conversation?"

Dee shook her head. "No. I could tell you raised your voice, though."

"I'll tell you later."

After the game, which they won five to zero, Dee sat next to Sara on the bench. Before she could ask, Izzy called out from the other end of the dugout. "So, are you two lovebirds an item?"

Sara stared at Izzy but didn't reply. Dee blushed.

Izzy followed up with a cat whistle.

"Have you ordered the U-Haul?" someone shouted.

"Very funny," Sara said.

"No," Mannie said. "They skipped the U-Haul."

"Shut it, Mannie," Sara said.

"What do you mean, order a U-Haul?" Dee said.

Mannie stared at Sara. Sara met her gaze but dropped it when Mannie shook her head.

"Divide and conquer?" Rose said, directing her comment to Mannie.

"I already tried talking to Sara," Mannie said, speaking as if Sara wasn't present.

"We don't need your advice, thanks," Sara said.

"Maybe you don't. But Dee does," Rose said.

"Dee," Rose said, inclining her head before heading out of the dugout.

Dee got the message and stood to follow Rose, who headed down the third-base line and into the outfield. She turned around when she was halfway between third base and the back fence.

"Are you okay? I heard about what happened with your parents. I'm so sorry."

"Thanks." Dee's eyes suddenly filled with tears. "I'm sorry. I don't know why I'm so emotional all of a sudden."

"It's okay. You're going through a lot."

Dee nodded as tears rolled down her cheeks. She wiped them away as if they were bothersome flies.

"What did you mean by divide and conquer?"

"Some of us on the team are worried that you and Sara may be moving too quickly."

Dee took a deep breath and let it out, along with more tears. "I really like Sara. And it's so nice to be with her. But I feel so out of place at her house."

"You can like her and want to be with her but not move in together."

"Is that why someone joked about a U-Haul?"

"There's a joke that makes fun of the fact that lesbians often move in together quickly. That we order a U-Haul on the second date."

"We haven't even had one date."

"No, you haven't."

"But I needed some place to stay."

"Yes, you did. And you still do." Rose paused. "Can I give you my advice?"

Dee nodded. "Please."

"I think you and Sara will have a better chance of making it if you don't live together right away. A lot has changed for you really quickly."

Dee let out a half laugh, half sob.

"If you really like Sara, don't rush into it. If it's meant to be, you'll be okay. But give yourself space to figure it out."

"I'm afraid if I say I want to live somewhere else that it will hurt her feelings."

"Sara's a big girl. But that you feel that way makes me wonder if you might not be doing things for the wrong reason. You don't want to live with someone to avoid hurting their feelings. That's not how to build a relationship."

"Where would I go?"

"My partner and I have an extra room you can stay in for six months if you want. It's enough time for you to get over this crazy period and find some place you want to live. And I also believe Mannie has an extra room she'll offer you."

"Mannie intimidates me."

"Aw, she just pretends to be tough."

"I'd like to stay with you if it's really okay."

"Absolutely."

"And you're sure your partner's okay with it?"

"Yep. Plus, we figure you'll probably spend a lot of time at Sara's. But this way you get to choose."

Dee smiled. "I like that."

Rose glanced over Dee's shoulder. She patted Dee on the shoulder as she started to walk back toward the dugout. "Good luck. I'll text you my address."

Why Rose said, "Good luck," became clear when Dee turned around. Sara was walking their way. Rose stopped her and Dee could hear her say, "She really likes you. Remember that."

Sara tilted her head. Her eyes scrunched together. Confused, she watched after Rose for a moment before turning to Dee.

"Hey, you okay?" Sara said, only just noticing the tears on Dee's cheeks. "You've been crying."

Dee nodded.

"What's wrong?"

Dee forced herself to meet Sara's gaze. "I really like you, Sara."

Seeing Sara's face drop like she'd been given devastating news, Dee quickly added, "And I want to be with you. I do."

"But?"

"It's all so fast. I've come home from work feeling lost and out of place. It's your house, Sara. And it's too quick for me to try and make it ours. I'm sorry."

"Why didn't you tell me?"

"Everything's been so crazy for me I haven't really known what I was feeling. And ..." Dee looked away before settling her gaze on the ground, "I was afraid of hurting your feelings. Of having you assume I didn't want to be with you. Which isn't the case at all. I just ... I want to be able to choose you. I want to choose when I come over and when I need to be in my own space."

The corner of Sara's mouth turned up. "I want you to be able to choose too." Sara glanced over her head. "Was that something Rose said?"

"Yeah."

"That Rose is pretty smart. Are you going to stay with her?"

"Yep. Are you sure you're okay with that?"

"Absolutely. If and when we move in together, let's have it be because we choose it, not because we don't think we have another option."

The two lovers stared into each other's eyes, smiled and embraced. They returned to the dugout hand in hand.

"So?" Mannie asked when they returned to the dugout to retrieve their equipment.

"So, we're going to slow it down a little," Sara said.

Mannie nodded. "I really think you too will have a better chance at making it."

"That's what Rose said," Dee said.

"Did you all talk ahead of time?" Sara asked.

"We may have ... planned an intervention," Mannie said. She smiled unapologetically. "It's what friends do when one of them does something crazy."

"Something crazy, huh?" Sara said.

"Yep." Mannie stared at Sara, waiting.

Sara nodded thoughtfully. "Thanks." She held out her hand, and Mannie grasped it.

Sara and Dee wandered back to Sara's car. "Let's get you packed up," Sara said.

"How about we do that tomorrow?" Dee said.

"You sure?" Sara asked.

"Yeah. Knowing I've got a place to go that's separate from yours makes it easier for me to be at your place. Does that make sense?"

"It does."

They held hands as Sara drove back to her house. It was a quiet drive, as both women were lost in their own thoughts. When Sara pulled up outside her house, she turned toward Dee, who was smiling and appeared more relaxed than she'd been in days. A weight she hadn't known she'd been carrying fell away. There were no guarantees, but Sara knew they stood a chance. She returned Dee's smile before getting out of the car and heading into the house, walking hand in hand with her new girlfriend.

Please click or copy and paste the link below to write a review for this book. Reviews are essential to an author's success. Without them, many people won't take a chance on a book. Thank you for taking that risk. If you could spend another minute writing a quick review or even just noting how many stars you think it deserves, I'd greatly appreciate it.

https://www.amazon.com/review/create-review/error?ie=UTF8&channel=glance-detail&asin=B0BLJDKJPX

Other Books by Sam Kestrel

About the Author

Sam Kestrel writes lesbian erotica, romance and mystery. Sam is a quiet, behind-the-scenes kind of gal and she can't actually believe that with this pen name, she had the guts to start writing erotica. Just another lesson in the universe having other ideas when we're off making plans. In her other life she writes children's books and figures that it's best to keep these pen names separate. Her writing journey started on Medium where she began with short stories limited to 2k words. But now she wants to write more complicated characters and stories and is shifting into longer works that will allow her to do that. Through her newsletter and website, samkestrel.com, Sam hopes to connect with her readers. She really wants you to drop her a line. No kidding. And newsletter subscribers get a free epilogue to Working From Home, a short story not available anywhere else.

You can connect with me on:

- https://samkestrel.com
- https://samkestrel555
- https://www.facebook.com/samkestrel555

Subscribe to my newsletter:

- https://samkestrel.com